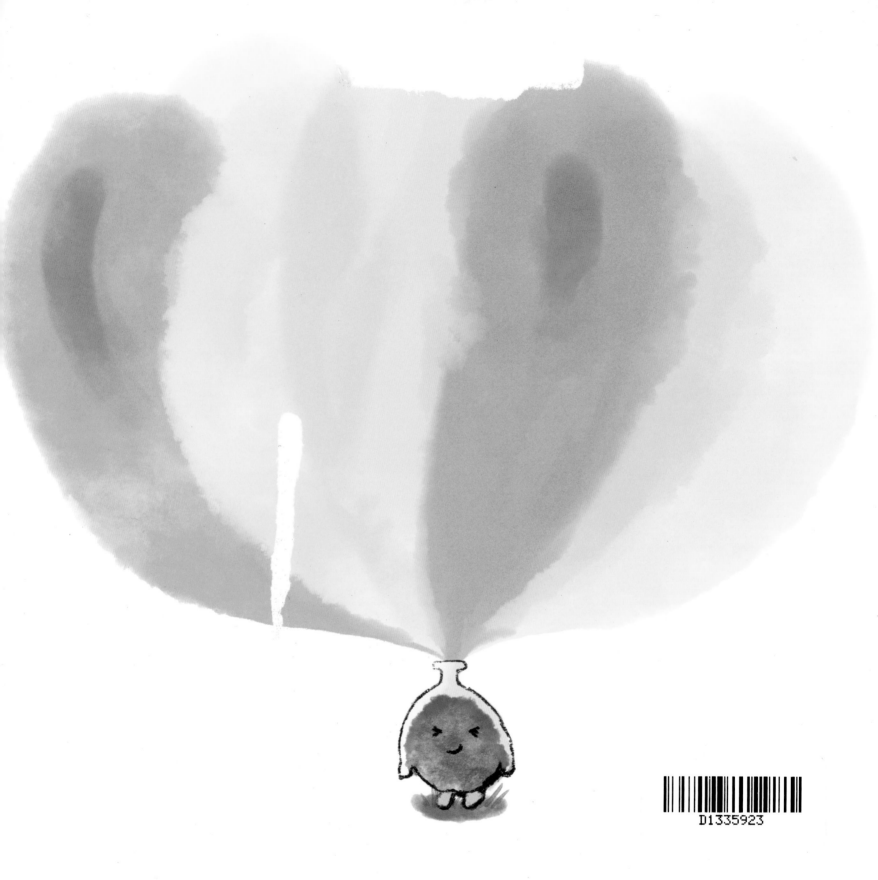

D1335923

For the are the Ploofers.
Mia

practising something really special.

They are going to...

But that's not all...

Are you ready?

Wait...
here it comes...

TA-DA!
They are flying!

He's still all the way down there!

Don't worry, little one!
We're coming back to get you.

Hey! Hop on!
Flying is amazing!

Um, it's OK, thank you.
I'll just wait down here.

That's alright.
You're missing out though.

Wheee!
Back up we go.

WOW!

The Ploofers are flying!
Don't you think it looks fun, little one?

Not really.
Being up there
looks way too scary.

How about if
I come with you?
I'll hold your hand
and we can be brave
together.

Mmm...
OK.

AHOY!
COME DOWN!
We're going to join you!

Come on,
you'll love it!

It's alright, little one.
You can do it.

Just take my hand...

NO,
I feel like a wobbly jelly!
I can't do it.

It's OK.
Everyone feels scared sometimes.

All you need is a little bit of **courage!**

Really?

Yes! Let's take it one step at a time...

First, make a little shoof...

then, turn upside down.

Now shoof a little more...

that's it! We're going up!

No!
I'm scared!

It's alright.

Let's try again...

up we go!

You're doing so
well - keep going!

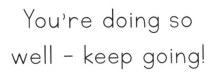

I feel so light and free...

as if I'm flying through the air!

Well...
you ARE flying through the air!

But don't worry - you're
full of courage now.

Actually,
I don't feel like
a jelly anymore...

I feel
brave.

Look, everyone is so proud of you!
Shall we go and join them?

Wow! It IS amazing up here!

With a little bit of courage, we can
go **anywhere** and do **anything**.